The CHESTER TOWN TEA PARTY

By Brenda Seabrooke

Illustrated by Nancy Coates Smith

Tidewater Publishers
Centreville, Maryland

Amanda Wetherby folded the feather mattress over on the bed. "I can carry it by myself," she told her older sister Prue. She was nine now and not a baby anymore. She didn't need help to carry the winter mattress to sun before storing it in the attic for the summer. She had already carried the summer mattresses of horsehair down from the attic and spread them over the lilac bushes.

She picked the mattress up. As she carried it to the door of the bedroom, it billowed and puffed around her. She hadn't expected it to be so bulky—she couldn't see where she was going. The heel of her shoe caught on the doorsill and she fell headfirst into the mattress and out into the hall. Her brother Gideon untangled her.

"It feels like a warm nest," she told him.

"And you look like a bedraggled baby bird," said her other brother George. Gideon helped Amanda carry the feather bedding out to the garden and spread it over the hedge. George followed with his pole and fishhooks.

"Why do I have to do chores while he gets to go fishing?" Amanda complained to Gideon. He was fifteen and already helping in their father's store. George was twelve and never seemed to do anything but fish and have fun.

"I've done my chores for the day," George said. "I got up early. Besides, you like to eat the fish and crabs I catch."

"I'd like to catch fish and crabs, too," Amanda said. "It's more fun than airing bedding."

"But you're not good at it the way I am," George said.

"I could be," Amanda said, "if I ever got a chance to practice."

But George was already out the gate. Gideon tweaked her brown curls. "Prue doesn't mind her work."

Amanda tossed her head. Prue was fourteen and practicing for her own home. "Prue likes housework. She loves to sun the bedding. She thinks it's fun."

Gideon laughed. "I'll take you fishing next week," he promised.

"Thank you, Gideon," Amanda said. But it was not the same as going fishing anytime she felt like it, the way George did.

For supper that night they had crab cakes that Prue made from the crabs George caught. Amanda had to admit they were delicious. She poured herself another cup of buttermilk and sipped it.

"I wish we had some tea," she said.

"It will be a long time before we have tea again in Chester Town," said Father, "after the town voted against buying and selling it. The British government must see that the colonies will not stand being treated like children, taxing us without representation in Parliament, closing our ports."

"What does that mean?" asked Amanda.

"The British government won't let us in the colonies send a representative to Parliament where the tax laws are made," said Father. "Parliament passed an unfair tax on tea. Some people in Boston dressed like Indians one night and dumped a shipload of tea into the harbor. To punish them the British won't allow ships to bring trade goods to or from Boston."

"I wish I'd been there when they dumped the tea in the harbor," George said with enthusiasm.

"What would you have done, George?" Gideon teased.

"I would have dressed like a Mohawk Indian. I would even have shaved my hair off the sides and painted my face. Like this." He dipped his finger into the blackberry juice and made purple lines on his cheeks and down his nose.

"George!" reproved his mother.

"That was not a dignified way to take a stand against an unfair tax," said Father.

"But the British should not have closed the port of Boston in retaliation," Gideon pointed out.

"Those poor people," said Mother. "I'm afraid many will suffer if ships aren't allowed in with provisions."

"But I still don't see why Chester Town had to ban tea," Amanda said. "How is that going to help Boston?"

"It shows that we are in sympathy with Boston," Prue said as she cleared the table.

Amanda was unconvinced. "What if Mr. Geddes unloads the tea on his ship and somebody sells it in his store?"

"Nobody in Chester Town will unload, sell, or buy the tea," said Father.

"But what will happen to it?" Amanda asked. "Will it stay in the ship forever?"

"No," said Gideon. "When the British understand that we mean what we say, Mr. Geddes will send the tea back to London."

"When will they understand?" Amanda asked.

"Ah, that is the problem," said Gideon.

The next day Mrs. Wetherby gave Amanda a list of chores. "Prue and I are going to Mrs. Gilchrist's to work on quilting all day. Be sure to weed the garden early, before the sun is hot, and wear your sunbonnet."

"I always do," Amanda said.

But she dawdled all morning. She drew pictures in the dirt with a stick, played with her cat, found a duck egg, chased a butterfly, and soon it was afternoon. She would have to weed in the sun.

Amanda sighed and went to the garden. She pulled up a weed. It was hot down in the rows of peas and beans. Maybe it would rain so she could quit. She looked up at the sky. There wasn't a cloud in sight. Amanda pulled another weed. She was already sweating. She wiped her face with the back of her hand. Dirt stuck to her cheek.

George came out of the house.

"Where are you going?" Amanda asked.

"To a tea party," he said with a grin.

"But Gideon and Father said there would be no tea in Chester Town for a long time," Amanda reminded him.

"Oh, there will be lots of tea at this party," George assured her.

"Can I come? I want some tea, too," she said.

"No girls allowed. This tea party is just for men." He stuck out his chest.

"Where is the tea party going to be?"

"It starts at the square," he said. The gate closed behind him with a clatter.

It wasn't fair. Yesterday George went fishing while she changed the mattresses. Today he was going to a tea party while she had to pull weeds. Amanda jerked another weed so hard it broke off. Now she would have to dig the root out.

She was hot and sweaty and thirsty.

Why couldn't she go to the tea party, too? If she were a boy she could go. Amanda jumped up. She could pretend to be a boy!

She ran into the house to the chest where her mother kept quilting material. She rummaged until she found an old pair of George's outgrown britches and a ragged shirt that hadn't been cut into quilt squares yet.

Amanda held them up against her. They looked the right size. Quickly, she untied the laces to her bodice, stepped out of her petticoat, and put on the shirt. The sleeves were too long so she rolled them to her elbows. The britches ended a little below her knees. She left on

her own stockings. Her leather shoes with the buckles on the front were almost like her brother's. They would have to do.

She clubbed her hair back with a string and looked at herself in the mirror. She thought she made a good boy. Nobody would notice her now except maybe George. She could fool him. All she had to do was swagger around the way he did and act like she owned the world.

Amanda hurried outside. She didn't want to be late. But the sun was warm on her cheeks. She had never been in the sun without her sunbonnet. Her face would soon be red without it. She didn't have a hat. What could she do?

She kicked at the dirt. She didn't dare let her face be burned by the sun. Already it felt gritty from her weeding, even though she had worn her sunbonnet.

That was the answer—dirt. Amanda scooped up a handful from between the bean rows and wiped her face with it. The dirt stuck to her sweaty skin, protecting it from the sun's rays. Now she was ready to go to the tea party. Nobody would ever think this dirty-faced boy was Amanda.

She ran down the garden path, feeling free without her petticoats flapping around her ankles. How nice it must be to be a boy sometimes, she thought.

As Amanda skipped down High Street, she wondered what kind of cakes they would have at the tea party. She hoped they would have her favorite crimson biscuits.

The square was filled with men and boys. They didn't notice when Amanda slipped in among them. She was looking for George and jumped when a red-faced man shouted, "That tea is an abomination!"

A tall, thin man nodded and said, "Amen." Clouds of white powder puffed out of his wig with every nod.

"An abomination, I say!"

"An insult to us as Englishmen," said a man in a snuff-colored coat.

"Amen," agreed the thin man, nodding.

His wig powder tickled Amanda's nose. She sneezed.

"Boston must be avenged!" someone yelled.

"Amen," nodded the thin man again. Amanda moved to get away from the puffs of powder. She bumped into a broad-shouldered man and looked up.

It was her father. Amanda slid farther into the crowd. Her father hadn't seen her. He was listening as the crowd grew noisier.

"We'll show those British we mean business!" shouted the red-faced man.

"To the wharf!" yelled a boy. Amanda was startled to see that it was George. She ducked behind another man as the crowd moved down High Street toward the wharf on the Chester River where she could see the brig *Geddes* moored.

Maybe that was where the tea party would be, Amanda thought as she went along with the crowd. She tripped over the cobblestones as she ran down the street yelling, "To the wharf!" as loud as she could. Amanda had never had so much fun.

The crowd ran out on the wharf and swarmed onto the *Geddes*.

"Let the fishes pay King George's tax!" shouted the red-faced man.

Boys jumped into the hold of the ship and hoisted up tea chests. Now they would have the party, Amanda thought as she climbed onto the ship.

She backed into someone and turned around. It was Gideon. George hadn't recognized her, but Gideon surely would. Amanda froze.

But Gideon only glanced at her and said, "Here, boy, help me with this chest."

Amanda didn't know what they were going to do with the chest but she took hold of one end as Gideon took the other.

"Heave!" Gideon said. They picked up the chest and swung it overboard. Amanda let go. The chest flew through the air and landed with a loud splash in the river. It floated for a minute, then sank in a trail of bubbles. Amanda saw George and a group of boys throw another chest into the water. Now she understood. It was that kind of tea party, the kind that Boston had had, not the kind with tea and cakes.

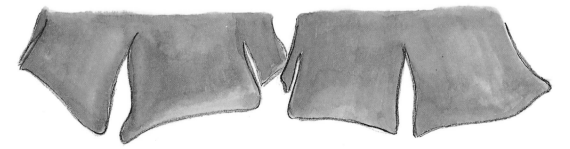

The men and boys cheered as the last tea chest
went overboard.

"Let us toast the fishes," said the fat man.

Everyone laughed and the crowd moved up the
street to Worrell's Tavern.

Amanda slipped away from the hubbub. She ran home and closed the gate softly behind her. Prue and Mother might be back by now. She would be in trouble if her mother found out what she had done.

She took her clothes into the well house and changed. She tied her hair into a clumsy knot and put her sunbonnet back on. Then she bundled George's clothes into an empty basket and pulled up a bucket of water.

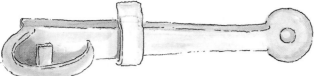

She was rinsing the dirt from her face when her mother said from the doorway, "There you are, Amanda. I was wondering where you had got to."

"Oh, I was so hot," Amanda said. "I came to cool my face off."

"You do look flushed," her mother said. "Come inside and rest this afternoon. The weeds can wait."

Amanda felt guilty for getting out of her work, so she spent the rest of the afternoon cutting quilting squares for her mother.

Her brothers came home full of news about the tea party. Gideon and Father had gone back to the store, but George had stayed at the tavern.

"Mr. Geddes was mad that his tea was dumped," George said.

"It was bound to happen," said Father. "Mr. Geddes should not have brought it here in these times. He knew the risk."

"Cefus Redding said this tea party was more important than the one in Boston," George said.

"Perhaps it was," said Father. "This one was held in support of Boston. It means the colonies are sticking together against the British."

"Yes, and our tea party happened in broad daylight," boasted George, "not at night like the one in Boston. *They* weren't as brave as we were. *They* dressed up like Indians. *We* didn't even disguise ourselves."

"No, indeed," Gideon said. "We marched down to the *Geddes* as the men and boys that we are, not a single disguise among us." He looked at Amanda and winked.

Amanda stared at Gideon. He knew! He had recognized her even with her disguise! But Amanda knew he would never tell.

"May 23, 1774. This is a date we will long remember," said Father.

Amanda knew that she would never forget it. It was the most exciting tea party she had ever been to.